A LITTLE CHRISTMAS DREAM
— DELILAH RICHARD

A Little
Christmas Dream

Delilah Richard

**Bibliographic information of the German
National Library:**
The German National Library lists this
publication in the German National Bibliography.
Detailed bibliographic data is available on the Internet at <u>dnb.dnb.de</u>

© 2024 Delilah Richard
Publisher: BoD · Books on Demand GmbH, In de Tarpen 42,
22848 Norderstedt
Printed by: Libri Plureos GmbH, Friedensallee 273,
22763 Hamburg
ISBN: 978-3-7693-1142-6

IN MEMORY OF MY GRANDPARENTS

3 days until Christmas

Every year, my grandma puts up the most beautiful Christmas tree in the whole neighborhood. It was already a tradition. This year I was alone, without my family. My grandma was already full of anticipation and had baked cookies. The whole house smelled of gingerbread, and all the rooms were decorated with golden slats.

All I could think about was that Christmas Day was finally coming, and I could unwrap my presents. This year, I wished for a PlayStation; my grandma and grandpa would fulfill my wish. Like every other wish I had. My mother was reluctant to leave me behind and wanted me to come with her to Florida, but I wanted to stay with my grandparents.

Christmas music was playing in the kitchen, and my grandma was singing along and enjoying the baking. The whole neighborhood was invited to the next day, and she would prepare a Christmas feast for them. I looked out of the window.

It was freezing outside and snowing. I saw children playing, building a snowman, and having a snowball fight. I blew on the window with all my might and wiped away the blurry shimmer to watch the children closely.

They were laughing and looking very happy, throwing snow at each other. Then the mother came and scolded the children. I giggled a little at myself. When suddenly the doorbell rang!

"I'm already opening for Grandma!"

"What are you saying, my child? I can't understand you!" I ran to the door as fast as I could, and when I opened it, I saw a Christmas tree in front of me. Furthermore, I was curious to see who was hiding behind it. As the tree seemed to move of its own accord, I saw my grandpa behind it, carrying it in with all his might. A wonderful blue spruce.

"Oh, child, please get out of the way. I can't see anything." "Grandpa, may I help you?"

"My child, please get out of the way. It's far too heavy. I think I'm going to fall." He carried it into the living room with the very last of his strength; meanwhile, my grandma had also noticed and came out of the kitchen cheerfully. She had a broad, relieved grin all over her face.

The tree had finally arrived. After all, it was already three days before Christmas, and tomorrow the whole neighborhood was invited along with the parents and children.

"Grandma, may I help you decorate the Christmas tree?"

"My child, I want you to rest and maybe play with the other children; what do you think?"

"But I don't want to play with the other children; I want to help you decorate the Christmas tree."

"Yes, we'll see. I still have so much to do, and I have to be systematic."

"Systematically?" I was a little offended that she couldn't give me an answer so quickly, as I really wanted to help her put up the Christmas tree. Likewise, I went back to the window and checked to see if the children were still having their snowball fight outside. There was no one to be seen.

Well, it was starting to get dark, and the children were bound to get into trouble with their mother. I was a little offended, I hid in the corner. My grandpa tried to fix the Christmas tree and cut it to size. The tree went up to the ceiling, and the top of the tree bounced off the ceiling stucco. The whole house had high, large, and bright windows. The house was brightly lit by the snow, and the smell of gingerbread was firmly anchored in my nose.

I loved the smell of freshly baked cookies. My grandma baked the best cookies. She still had three more cakes in the oven; my grandma was overworking herself, like every year. I really wanted to help her with the preparation. But she refused to be helped. She seemed very happy to do her work alone.

"Grandpa, can I help you with the Christmas tree?" He looked relatively speechless in the air and whispered something to Grandma. Grandma's laughter changed to a gloomy face, and they both started a discussion. I was still offended that no one could give me a proper answer. Not even decorated yet, the Christmas tree just looked fantastic. I tried one last time and went to my grandma's.

"Grandma, are you sure I can't help you with something?" "Please, we have a lot to do here. Why don't you go into the kitchen and try my homemade cake that I made yesterday?

I also made chocolate cake. I know it's your favorite." I resigned myself to this answer. It was slowly getting dark, and I ventured into the living room again. I didn't see anyone, just the Christmas tree in the middle of the room. Then I walked through the house to the dining area, where the whole table was beautifully decorated, with gold and red Christmas decorations spread out perfectly on the table.

The whole house was glowing with lights. It was just perfectly set. Had my grandma done everything on her own? I felt bad that I only ate my chocolate and couldn't help my grandma and grandpa. Nevertheless, it was simply wonderful and fantastic, and I was eagerly waiting for the next day when the whole neighborhood would come to visit. My grandma finally joined us.

"Grandma, did you do all this on your own? It just looks incredible! But I wanted to help you!"

She placed name cards on the table. Grandma had thought of everything. I know she still had three cakes in the oven.

"I know, my child, that you want to help me, but you know, Grandma, I really, really like doing it all on my own, then I'll finish it faster. Please don't be offended. Just enjoy the holidays with us, we'll do the rest."

She gave me a kiss on the cheek and continued to decorate the table. I finally resigned myself to having nothing to do and went to my room to recover a little from all the impressions, and my anticipation for Christmas grew more and more. I tossed and turned in bed and couldn't sleep because of the excitement.

Would Grandma be asleep too? What is Grandpa doing? Who is decorating the Christmas tree? It's only two days until Christmas. I looked at the clock, and it was already 1 AM. I counted the sheep so I could finally fall asleep. And it worked. I entered the world of dreams...

2 days until Christmas

When I woke up the next morning, the sun was beating down on my face with all its might. I jumped out of bed excitedly and ran to the window. The snow was scattered in the front garden of the house. A snowman was looking at me. I grinned a little and thought about the children from the day before. Maybe they will come tonight too! I was so excited and happy and ran into the living room in my pajamas. Surely, I could finally decorate the Christmas tree with my grandpa and grandma today.

When I got to the living room, I saw a fully decorated Christmas tree that couldn't shine any brighter. The face of the tree made me sad and happy at the same time. The tree was decorated with golden balls, numerous lights, and slats, and as a tradition, the tree had a big golden star on the top. I don't think I've ever seen a more beautiful Christmas tree like this one. At the bottom of the tree, everything was covered in absorbent cotton. There was a little house on top, inside was a crib and the baby Jesus.

There was a nutcracker, angels, and lots of wrapped presents with gold, silver, and red wrapping paper. I ran as fast as I could to the gifts and tried to shake them a little. Carefully, of course, there could be glass inside! I looked closely at each present and analyzed the shape of the package. Maybe my PlayStation was in there too. I had a package that was shaped like a PlayStation. I wanted to unpack the package immediately and start playing. But I had to be patient. There were only two days until Christmas Eve. I had completely lost track of time with all the presents. I looked around and didn't see anyone, maybe I should start getting changed as the guests would be arriving soon! Not only that, but I ran into the kitchen, and there was no one there either.

Then I went to the dining area. There was no one there either! The whole house smelled of chocolate cake and tangerines. How I loved that smell. I ran out to the front door to the underground garage in my pajamas. The car was gone.

The only thing I saw was the snowman and the children opposite, laughing at me because I was still in my pajamas. It was freezing cold. It didn't stop snowing. The snow was 20 cm thick. The cars were snowed in, and it was very slippery. I decided to go back into the house quickly.

Had I possibly overslept for the day? Maybe my grandparents decided to go to the neighbors' house? And left me alone? I don't think so. I went back to the dining area to make sure everything was still there. Fortunately, I breathed a sigh of relief. All the decorated dishes and name tags were still on the table. I was suddenly overcome by a smell. I followed it into the kitchen. There was a giant turkey sizzling away.

My mouth was watering, it looked so delicious. I was amazed at what my grandmother could still conjure up. And again, I felt bad that I couldn't help her with anything! I looked at the clock and quickly ran to my room to get ready, as guests could arrive at any time. It would be embarrassing if I were still walking around in my pajamas. I put on my red dress, which my mother had bought me on purpose for Christmas. I combed my hair and put it up in an updo. My favorite perfume was a must, as were my necklace and earrings and, of course, my best shoes. The radiance on my face was impossible to miss. Finally, I heard my grandma and grandpa drive into the underground parking garage. They were talking and unpacking something from the trunk. I looked out of the window and called out to them.

"There you are at last! I thought you'd forgotten about me." They both laughed and grinned to themselves. "Hello, my child, we had to do some shopping."

"You call that some shopping? Did you buy the whole store empty?" "You never know who else will come along."

"Yeah, I agree." I took a bag from my grandma and put it in the kitchen. "Oh my God, the turkey, is the turkey burned?" "Tell me, Grandma, how did you manage to set the whole table, decorate the Christmas tree so beautifully, and get another turkey in the oven?" Grandpa came into the kitchen with the rest of the bags.

"Well, that's how your grandma is, she doesn't let anyone talk her into her work, nor does she let anyone help her, but then you see the result and accept that she can do it better on her own!" Grandma smiled contentedly at my grandpa. "What else did you buy?"

"Well, you know, we bought some chocolate for the children who might be coming, then I bought another cake to keep in stock."

"Oh, and the three cakes aren't enough?"

"I can't cater to everyone's taste!"

"Yes, you really have thought of everything." Grandpa sorted the things into the fridge, put the cake on a plate, and finished it off. Grandma investigated the oven and looked a little nervous. "What do you think, darling, will the turkey be ready before the guests arrive?" Grandpa just shook his head. We all started laughing. But Grandma couldn't be stopped, she ran excitedly back and forth from the kitchen to the dining area to put the starters on the table. The guests could be at the door any minute. Her polished silver cutlery shone in competition with the lights on the Christmas tree. When else had she managed to polish her cutlery?

There wasn't another granny like her. I was glad to be here. But I was still standing around in the middle of the house and didn't know how I could help my grandma. She brought candles to the table, lit them, and sprinkled an orange scent all over the house. I didn't want to get in the way anymore, so I went into the living room and sat down next to the tree to continue analyzing the presents.

There were no more presents! Were there no presents this year? Grandma came with large packages that looked like Christmas presents. She put down a boot wrapped in chocolate. There were tangerines in another. Next to it was a nutcracker and plenty of sweets.

"Grandma, are these my presents?"

"They're presents for the neighbor's children. It's our tradition to have a feast with the neighbors two days before Christmas. The actual presents are distributed on Boxing Day."

"What kind of tradition is that?"

I wondered.

"Well, our tradition! Since most of the neighbors are with their other families at Christmas or on Christmas Day, we've made it a point among ourselves to organize this feast two days before Christmas. And you know I enjoy playing host, I love putting up my Christmas tree and cooking for everyone. It's the most wonderful time of the year." She hugged me and gave me a big kiss on the cheek. Her hands smelled of tangerines. "Grandma, have you been eating mandarins?"

"Yes, I was so hungry, but I would rather not eat now before the guests arrived. Please don't bother me anymore, they'll be here in an hour." I didn't know what else she wanted to do, as everything already looked perfect to me. The name tags were in place. It smelled of mint, lemon, and oranges in the whole house. Everything was polished down to the smallest corner.

The candles were lit, and the turkey was ready on the table. Potatoes and vegetables. The sight of it only made me hungrier. But I had to be patient, I wasn't allowed to eat anything yet or look for my presents, and I couldn't help anyone. Christmas music was on. Lights were lit all around the house. Grandpa had taken care of that!

The nutcracker was shining under the Christmas tree. Even the light was on in the little house where the crib and baby Jesus stood. It was wonderful. And how could it be otherwise? It was starting to snow outside. It already felt like Christmas! But the pre-Christmas period is even more beautiful than Christmas itself.

Anticipation of spending the festive season with your loved ones is the most precious gift you have in life. Having pondered enough, I walked back to the window. I took a corner of my dress and wiped the window clean. I wondered if the snowman was still there. The snowman was looking at me when suddenly a snowball hit my window. Where did it come from? I opened the window, but there was no one there.

I looked to the left. I looked to the right. Suddenly, a gigantic snowball hit my face. I was so annoyed and so shocked that I immediately grabbed my jacket and went outside to see who had thrown a snowball in my face. "Hey, show yourself. Do you think that's funny? Well, wait until I find you." I went to the snowman, bent down and kneaded a snowball. It was so cold. I wasn't even wearing gloves! And to make matters worse, it was snowing! As I knelt down, another snowball hit me on the back. "Well, wait, I'll get you yet."

"Try your luck."

"Who said that?" I ran around the house. "Whoever you are, I'm going to get you." Suddenly, I slipped. I screamed over the whole neighborhood. Then someone came to help. "Oh, sorry, I didn't mean to do that."

A girl helped me up. I was covered in snow, and I was terribly cold. "Who are you?"

"I live in the neighborhood. My mother and my grandmother are friends."

"So, you're invited to dinner with us today, and then you throw a snowball in my face?"

"Well, you looked so thoughtful, I wanted to have a little fun. I'm sorry. I didn't know you were going to be so angry or hit the floor."

"Yeah, I didn't know that either."

"Oh well, never mind." She held out her hand, wanting to bury the hatchet. "Friends?" I hesitated briefly, took the snowball I had hidden behind my back, and threw it full force into her face. She was so angry. I laughed and ran to the front door. "Wait a minute," she shouted.

She ran after me. Grandma opened the door. "But kids, what are you doing? Come in, it's far too cold! Marie-Therese, I'm glad to see you here, are your parents coming too?"

"Yes, Mrs. Richard, is Mr. Richard here too?"

"Of course, Marie, come in, my goodness, you've got snow all over your coat. What's happened?"

Marie and I looked at each other, puzzled. "I can see you've gotten to know each other."

"Yes, Grandma, we have!"

"All right, I have to get on with it now, the guests could arrive any minute." My grandma ran into the kitchen faster than lightning again. Marie and I scowled at each other.

Hang on, there'll be a sequel, I thought to myself. My grandpa came up to Marie-Therese and hugged her. "Hello, my darling, I'm so glad you made it."

"Yes, I'm happy to be here too."

"Have you got to know each other yet?"

"Yes, Grandpa, we have."

"Then just spread out around the house, and preferably don't help Grandma. Marie, you know she wants to do everything on her own. We'll stay out of everything and sit quietly at the table. What do you think?"

"But I need a minute to freshen up, I'll be right there."

I went into my room and took off my jacket to wash off the snow and put some makeup on my face.

I had finally warmed up a bit. But not enough. I was still angry with Marie-Therese. In the dining area, I warmed my hands by the fire, she had even thought of that! Everything was just perfect!

The scent of lemon, orange, and mint was in the air, every-where. Marie came over to me by the fire to warm her hands too. She whispered to me, "You know we still have a score to settle."

"Yes, I guess you're right."

"Okay, our accounts are balanced."

"What kind of accounts?"

"It's just a figure of speech, Marie." She looked at me a little miffed and turned her head towards the fireplace.

By now, the whole table was full of food. From salads, to Turkey, potatoes, mash, and venison.

I couldn't decide what to eat first. The fire was flickering in the fireplace, and Christmas music was playing. The Christmas tree shone brightly against the snow outside.

The blue spruce shone over the whole house and the whole neighborhood. "I just realized I don't even know your name."

"My name is Melissa."

"Nice to meet you, Melissa."

"Where are your parents, Marie?"

"I was wondering the same thing. I think they wanted to get some presents at the last minute." She put her hand over her mouth. "Oops, you're not supposed to say that! I must be putting my foot in my mouth every minute.

We got off to such a strange start, but I'm still glad you're here."

"I'm glad to be here too, Melissa."

"Sorry about that weird start. You were right, it's not such a great feeling to get a snowball in the face.

But your face looked funny doing it." I gave her a dirty look. "Come on, let's go to the table, let's see where our men's cards are."

"Oh, look, Melissa, what a coincidence. We're sitting next to each other. That's what I call a twist of fate."

"That could be it too." We took a seat at the table. Finally, the doorbell rang. My grandma took off her apron and ran excitedly to the door. She warmly greeted all the guests who came in. To my astonishment, they had all arrived at the same time. My grandpa took off the guests' coats and put them in the guest room. A dog ran towards me. It stuck its head out and wanted me to stroke its head. Who did this dog belong to? I asked myself quietly. My grandma was beaming all over her face. But she still wouldn't even let me help her now. She ran like a madwoman between the kitchen and the dining area. She looked back and forth nervously, wanting to please everyone, she was immensely popular with the guests. Everyone had a gift in their hand, which they gave to my grandma. The guests looked at the name cards to find their names. The dog was still there, and Marie Therese's parents had finally arrived. "Hello, my darling, is everything all right?" The mother greeted Marie-Therese. "Have you made any friends yet?" Marie-Therese nodded and gave her mother a kiss on the cheek. She sat down next to us. "You must be Mrs. Richard's granddaughter!" She hugged me warmly! "What's that cute dog? Is it yours?"

"Unfortunately, not." When almost everyone had gathered at the table, a boy suddenly came up to me. "Hello, I'm Philipp. I'm sorry, my dog, he just runs everywhere and always wants to be stroked. But apparently, he likes you."

"Yes, I think he's adorable too." My cheeks flushed a little. My cheeks took on the color of my dress. Marie-Therese noticed and laughed. "Philipp, I'm Melissa."

"How come we haven't met before?" asked Philipp. "That's a fair question," I replied. "Well, in any case, if my dog likes you, then of course I like you too." I looked over at him, confused. Was that a compliment now? "Thank you for the great compliment." I also looked over at Marie-Therese, a little confused. Meanwhile, Marie-Therese was laughing her head off. She could no longer hold back her loud laughter. She stretched her hand out to me and said, "I'm Marie-Therese, by the way. A very close friend of Melissa's!" Philipp was a little irritated. "Yes, hello Marie-Therese, I'm Philipp, and of course, I'm excited to meet you too."

"We can play snowball fight later if you like!"

"Yes, Marie, Melissa, will you join us then?"

"Yes, I think so," Marie-Therese grinned. "Well, it was a pleasure to meet you, I'll see you that evening. Come on, Grumpy." Philipp took his dog, Grumpy, and ran upstairs. If Grandma could see that. But Marie-Therese just couldn't help it; she grinned at me and said, "And we can play snowball fights together later; how red you've become. The blush outshines the color of your dress."

"Hahaha, Marie, that's not funny."

"Yes, it is."

"Now stop it."

"Okay, I've hit the bull's eye, you like Philipp."

"No, that's not true at all. What was that all about? If my dog likes you, do I like you too?"

"Well, that's a compliment, I don't know what's wrong with you. I can see the wedding coming." I slapped Marie-Therese on the shoulder. "Give it a rest! And besides, who calls their dog Grumpy?"

"Why not?"

"Could it be that you like Philip?"

"Oh, nonsense, what would it matter? I can see that he likes you! Now you're blushing again." Meanwhile, the music went off. By now, everyone was gathered around the table. There must have been around 30 people. Marie and I were so engrossed in conversation that we didn't even notice. Philipp was also sitting at the table. His dog is next to him. Marie Therese's father raised his glass in a toast.

"Please pay attention. Please be quiet for a moment, Marie, that goes for you too." Marie suddenly fell silent. "On behalf of my family, I would like to thank Mr. and Mrs. Richard for this invitation. We have been neighbors for years now and have this wonderful tradition of being able to meet in this house two days before Christmas Eve every year. I would like to thank the hosts from the bottom of my heart. I can only compliment the hostess once again on the remarkable and sensational things she has conjured up here.

Where is she? Melissa, can you go and get her?" I blushed again as everyone's eyes went from the table to me. I nodded sheepishly. Then I ran into the kitchen and, of course, saw my grandma excitedly and nervously working away in the kitchen. She was finishing the icing on the lemon meringue cake. It smelled of lemon, cream, and Mandarins. I didn't even know which smell I liked better. My grandma outdid herself again. "Grandma!" "Yes, my darling?" "The guests are waiting for you!" "Yes, but you can see I haven't finished the cake yet." "Grandma, a suggestion. You show me how it works, and I'll finish it for you, meanwhile, please go into the dining room and celebrate." "Celebrate me? For what?" I shook my head. "

You're far too modest. Look what a feast you've conjured up all by yourself." She had a little smile on her face. "Now take off your apron and go to your guests."

"But" … "No arguments." I took off her apron and sent her out of the door. "But only if you do me a favor."

"Which one again?"

"Only if you're there." She hugged me. "Of course." We went to the table together, where everyone was already waiting for us. "Finally, we thought you weren't coming. I wanted to tell you again in front of the whole team that every year you conjure up the most wonderful pre-Christmas celebration my family and I could have dreamed of.

We thank you very much for this and appreciate you as the very best neighbor we can have in the world. So, enough words, let's finally start eating!" People laughed and applauded him loudly. My grandma had tears in her eyes, she looked so happy. My grandpa cut open the turkey and gave each guest a piece.

It was a wonderful pre-Christmas atmosphere. Everyone at the table suddenly went quiet as they tasted the food. No matter what I ate, it tasted like a five-star restaurant. No one could have done it better. Everyone was eating except my grandma, of course, she couldn't stay seated and went back into the kitchen to finish the lemon meringue pie. It was just hopeless!

She wouldn't just stay at the table to enjoy the feast with her guests. After the first course, my grandma cleared everything away. The atmosphere was exuberant, and people started chatting. They laughed, sang, and enjoyed the feast. The children went to the Christmas tree to unwrap their presents. I didn't quite understand, as it wasn't Christmas yet. But apparently it was a tradition in this neighborhood to give each other small gifts before Christmas Eve. I was a little sad that I wasn't allowed to unwrap mine yet.

But I have to be patient. The fire in the fireplace flickered, and Christmas music played. Grumpy came to me again and wanted to be stroked. He just liked me. There was no sign of Philipp.

Marie-Therese had also disappeared. I ran to the window where the snowman was standing with his carrot, and there I saw the two of them throwing snow at each other! Now, I was offended that they were playing without me. I put on my winter coat and thick gloves.

Grumpy followed me unobtrusively. What a cute dog, I thought to myself. I took his lead and attached Grumpy to it to go out and disturb them. Outside, I walked around the whole house looking for them. I took a snowball. There was no sign of them.

When suddenly another snowball hit me on the back! "Ha, ha, ha, and I've got you again."

"Marie. Didn't we agree to let you do that? Well, wait, revenge is coming fast."

I took the snowball and ran after her. "Grumpy." Philipp ran after me. I ran after Marie. "Melissa, Melissa, why don't you stop?"

"Yes, Philipp."

"Why don't you stop?"

"Yes, that's all right."

"You seem to be having a lot of fun out here." "Yes, Melissa, you know Marie, she just made me. I asked for you, but she said she didn't know where you were. Well, my little Grumpy. My Grumpy and you really like each other. Like I said, if my dog likes you, I like you too." I looked a little embarrassed at the floor. Philip bent down to his dog to shake the snow off his head.

"What, am I stepping on your toes? If I say that sentence?" "Well, I don't know if that's a compliment, but if my dog likes you, I like you too!"

"Melissa, think about it, it's a fantastic sign when a dog likes you."

"Why is that?"

"You know, a person's best friend is still their dog! And if dogs like you, then you must be a good person!"

"Oh, that's what you mean!"

"What did you think I meant?" I turned around and wanted to change the subject. "Where is Marie anyway?"

"I don't know."

"I'm glad we're alone."

"Why is that?"

"Because I've wanted to do this all along!" He gave me a kiss on the cheek and threw a snowball in my face. I didn't know how to react, or why I had received a second snowball in my face within a day. Should I be happy about the kiss or irritated? I took as much snow in my hand as I could and threw the snowball into his face.

We continued to fight on the ground and argued about who should get more snow. Grumpy just watched us quietly. He looked at us wide-eyed in amazement. Music was playing from the house. My grandpa, who was excellent at playing the guitar, started to play his best pieces. Philipp and I were lying in the snow. Grumpy was still standing next to us. He started barking.

"I think we should go in!"

"Yes, Philipp, that's a good idea! I'm so cold." Philipp helped me up, took off his jacket, and put it over my shoulder. My whole dress was covered in snow. We went back into the house together. All the people were gathered around my grandpa singing Christmas carols.

Even my grandma. The presents were unwrapped, people were full, and four different cakes were on the table. Marie came up to us.

"Where have you been? You're covered in snow. Have you been having a snowball fight and didn't tell me?" Philipp and I looked at each other. "Okay, what happened? What did you do?"

"Nothing, Marie, we had a snowball fight, and you weren't there," I said cheekily. "I need to go to my room for a minute, Marie, to dry off the snow." In my room, I saw my door open. Grumpy had followed me again. I dried myself off a bit. My face also needed some powder.

My hands were still frozen from the snow. Back with the guests, I saw how everyone was celebrating the party and dancing to my grandpa's music. Marie and Philipp, too. I sat down at the table and tucked into the lemon meringue pie. It was delicious. A wonderful pre-Christmas celebration. It got later and later. The clock struck midnight. My grandma and grandpa said goodbye to the first guests. As the children had already had to sleep for a long time.

Marie had to go too. "Melissa, come here!" She hugged me. "It was a pleasure to meet you! I hope we meet again soon. Occasionally, the best friendships come from first funny impressions. What do you think?" Marie asked me. I smiled and immediately took her to my heart. "Marie, you're all right. And be prepared for something at our next meeting. There will be a rematch."

"Melissa, but for sure." She smiled and put on her jacket. I went to my room for a moment to relax a bit when my door opened again. "Grumpy, what's going on again?"

"I'm not Grumpy. Even though I might look a bit like him." I turned around, and in front of me was not Grumpy, but Philip. "Oh, it's you." I blushed all over my face again. Was there any way to turn something like that off? "Okay, I thought you were Grumpy."

"Do I walk exactly like Grumpy?"

"No, but you huff and puff just the same." Philip laughed. "I just wanted to say goodbye. We're going home so slowly, but if you like, we can write to each other. Do you want to?" I hesitated briefly. "But if you don't want to, of course, that's fine too. My dog can be wrong, too."

"No, I want to write to you."

"Okay, that, I'm glad. I'll leave you my number here," Philipp stuttered a little excitedly. He took a piece of paper out of his jacket pocket. He placed the piece of paper on my bedside table.

"Okay, Melissa, I'll be happy if you get in touch with me. And Grumpy will be happy too." He put Grumpy on the leash. "So, dear Grumpy, say goodbye to Melissa. He likes you very much. And I really like you, too. So, by the way." Philip looked at the floor. Grumpy was getting a little impatient. I blushed again, and Philip gave me a little kiss on the lips. When he walked out, I threw myself into my bed with joy and the snow-smeared dress.

I was so happy. It was my first kiss. There was no better moment than that. I put on my pajamas and went into the kitchen to check if my grandma was still there. In fact, she was still in the kitchen doing the dishes. My grandpa helped her diligently. "My darling, did you like it?"

"Yes, Grandma, it was just wonderful."

"Yes, I had the impression that you had made a new friend, Marie-Therese. I'm very happy, her parents have been our friends for years. And you can come and meet with Marie at any time."

"Yes, I will definitely do that."

"Yes, and the little boy too, what was his name, Philipp?" "I think his name is Philipp, and the little dog is called Grumpy."

"Grumpy?" My grandma looked at my grandfather. "Yes, that's right." I gave my grandma a kiss on the cheek. "Well, I'm very, tired now, and I'm going to go to sleep. Unless you want me to help you with the washing up?"

"Well, you know what the answer to that is," said Grandpa. "Yes, I know it." I went to sleep and dreamt of what was probably the best pre-Christmas party I've ever had in my life…

One day left until Christmas

The next morning, I woke up overjoyed. I looked at my bedside table, and there was the note from Philipp. Had I just dreamed it all, or was it the best evening of my life so far? I got out of bed to see what a wonderful thing Grandma had created again. Of course, the table was spotless, just as I always knew from my grandma. A breathtaking breakfast was laid out, with everything my heart desired. Freshly squeezed orange juice was on the table, and it smelled of coffee. She put out ginger, honey, and lemon tea for me.

"My darling, good morning!" My grandpa greeted grandma with a kiss on the cheek and sat down at the breakfast table in his pajamas. He picked up his morning newspaper and drank his coffee with relish. It was an incredible morning, and Christmas was just one day away. I was delighted. The Christmas tree still impressed me! The remains of the lemon meringue cake were also on the table.

The whole house still smelled of mandarins and mint. I decided to write to Philipp. Or was it far too soon, after one day? I had no experience and no one I could ask. But there was one person

I could ask, Marie—Therese. I was thickly wrapped up, this time with gloves and a hat, and definitely no dress under my thick winter coat. I trudged through the 20 cm of snow. The streets were empty, and it was very slippery. I knocked on the door. "Oh, hello Melissa, right?"

"Yes, exactly, EM, would it be possible to speak to Marie—Therese?"

"Yes, I'll get her, or you can come in. However, you like." "All right, I'll wait for her outside!"

"Marie, you have a visitor!" I waited outside the house, a cold wind was blowing, and I raised my hands in front of my face to blow in some warmth. "Hey." Marie had another snowball in her hand and was about to throw it at me. "I'm warning you, this time I'm prepared."

"What is it, so urgent?"

"Well, how can I put it into words?" I looked at her a little irritated. She laughed mischievously. "Spit it out, you know you can tell me anything."

"It's about, well, how can I put this? He gave me a little kiss and left his number on my bedside table. He wrote it on the piece of paper here. Now, I don't know if it's too early for me to get in touch with him today." Marie-Therese jumped for joy and hugged me. "Oh my God, I knew it. When he said, if my dog likes you, I like you too. From then on, I knew he liked you."

"Well, at least one of us knew!"

"Oh, don't be so pessimistic and just call him!"

"Today already?"

"Yes, when else, next year? Who knows what next year will be? Who knows what tomorrow is? Wait here."

Marie—Therese ran into the house. I ran up and down. Now it was starting to snow. It was actually wonderful for a walk with Philipp. I turned around and saw Marie coming towards me. With a phone in her hand. "What are you do-ing?"

"Here, I've already dialed the number you gave me."
"Wait, no, hang up."

"Why?"

"Hello, hello, who is this? Well, if no one answers, I'll hang up now."

"Wait, hello Philipp, it's me."

"Who, me?"

"Em, this is Melissa."

"Oh hi, I wasn't expecting you so early, not at all actually, to be honest." I gave Marie an annoyed look. Marie skillfully ignored it and prompted me to continue. "No, why shouldn't I get in touch with you?"

"Well, maybe I was too pushy for you."

"No, you weren't." Philip didn't say anything, and I blushed again. Marie was grinning all over her face. "Why I'm calling, well, I thought we could go for a walk in an hour or so."

"Yes, I'm in, and I'm bringing Grumpy with me."

"Great, see you around." I hung up. "Did I hang up too quickly? He didn't even say goodbye. What do you think?"

"I think you shouldn't worry too much and go home and warm yourself up by the fire and eat a piece of cake to calm your nerves. That's what I think!"

"You're the best!" I hugged Marie. "Oh, here, your phone."
"Yes, I think my mother still needs it." I was beaming all over my face. When I unlocked the door to the house, there was a big chocolate cake on the table.

My grandma was in the kitchen, my grandpa was reading his newspaper by the fireplace and smoking a cigar. "Everything's okay, you're beaming all over your face."

30

"Yes, Grandpa, I'm just happy to be here, it's such a lovely time with you. Is Grandma still baking and preparing?"

"Yes, you know her, where else would she be but baking in the kitchen?"

"All right, I'll go to my room, and then I'll go outside to get some fresh air." An hour later, there was a knock at the front door. I quickly ran to the front door so that my grandparents wouldn't find out about the meeting. I was a little embarrassed. "I'm off." My grandpa didn't even notice and was engrossed in his newspaper and what must have been his second or third cigar. Gone was the scent of gingerbread, cinnamon, and orange.

I opened the door, and Philipp was standing in front of me with Grumpy on the lead. Grumpy wanted to come to me straight away. Philipp was still holding him on the lead. I was also happy to see Grumpy again. It was snowing. The view of the street was beautiful. The snow was glistening in all its glory. Luckily, I was wearing thick gloves. Philipp took my hands and held them tightly.

Grumpy wriggled around my feet. "Come on, I'll warm your hands." He took off my gloves and warmed my hands and looked me in the eye, making me a little embarrassed and looking at the floor.

I put my gloves back on and took Grumpy by the leash. You could still see my grandparents' Christmas tree from outside. It lit up the whole neighborhood. "Come on, let's go for a walk." Philipp followed me with Grumpy.

"You're really lucky to have a home like this, your grandparents are fantastic."

"I know that, and I'm thankful for that every day. I couldn't be happier at the moment."

"And that's just to do with your grandparents, or are there other reasons?"

"Well, it's Christmas, the best time of the year, so I'm always happy, you know!" Philipp looked down at the ground, a little disappointed. We walked through the snow for a while, past a church with a choir singing Christmas carols in front of it. We had nothing to say to each other for a while. "How come…"

"What …"

"No, you first, Melissa."

"How come I didn't see your parents yesterday?" Philip swallowed hard. "Oh, sorry, I didn't mean to hit a sore spot with you!"

"No, that's okay. Well, my parents are usually away on business trips, and they don't want their pubescent son with them. I could mess up their important business and disturb them. You know, Melissa, not everyone is as lucky as you are to have such a sheltered home." We stopped a little at the church and listened to the choir. "I'm sorry about that, it sounds a bit lonely."

"Yes, a little, that's why this is already one of the best Christmases I've had. I'm so grateful that your grandma invited me to the party yesterday."

"It's also the best Christmas I've had so far," I said hesitantly. We walked back slowly. It was snowing harder and harder. You could still see my grandparents' Christmas tree from outside. We stopped in front of my grandparents' house.

I knelt down to stroke Grumpy on the head. Philip smiled mischievously. "Why are you smiling?"

"Grumpy just loves you, I've never seen him like this before!"

"You mean with a girl."

"I mean in general." Grumpy yowled a little impatiently.

We hugged and said goodbye. I walked quietly through the front door. It was now late evening. The tree was still glowing in different colors. My grandpa had fallen asleep in front of the fireplace with his newspaper on his knees. The fire was still on. I was just about to take the newspaper away from him when he woke up. "Oh, Melissa, I didn't hear you come in. Have you been out walking for so long? All alone? Isn't it too cold? It's all snowed over! I hope you haven't caught anything."

"No, Grandpa, everything's fine."

"To be honest, I wasn't alone, don't worry."

"Who were you with? I'd like to know now."

"With Philipp."

"Oh, well, then I don't have to worry."

"No, you don't have to."

"Where's Grandma?"

"She's asleep, she wasn't feeling too well and has gone to bed."

"What's wrong?"

"Well, she always has such bad headaches, and then she takes such strong medication for them. I'm always a bit worried and tell her, no, darling, maybe sometimes she can man-

age without medication, you know she doesn't listen to anyone. She's stubborn and will always be stubborn." Suddenly,
my grandfather becomes melancholy.

"I remember it like it was yesterday when I saw her for the
first time."

"Tell me about it."

"I don't want to bore you with my stories."

"You're not boring me with them, I'm listening." He picked
up the picture that was on the mantelpiece. It was the picture
of him and Grandma from their wedding day. "Where was
the picture taken?"

"It was in Hawaii, that's where we met for the first time,
your grandma and me." He added some wood and began to
tell the story of his life…

Time travel

I was a young and handsome marine soldier. We were stationed at the naval base in Hawaii. The mood among us soldiers was a bit downbeat. Still, life had to go on, and we had a worldwide deployment and stopped in Hawaii. My friend Mike was always, as we said at the time, on the lookout for a bride and was a Casanova in the greatest degree. He fell in love with every woman who crossed his path. I was the quieter of the two of us and was very relaxed and a good-natured contemporary.

I can still see it before my eyes as if it were yesterday. A wonderful evening under the starry Hawaiian sky. All the soldiers gathered for an after-work drink. A bar near the most beautiful beach in Hawaii. Mike and I had reserved the best spot on the stage with our comrades, where there was a little show that had a lot to offer. Mike nudged me and directed me to the two girls, who looked very neat and well groomed. A black-haired woman and a blonde woman. "Look, Richard, I'd like that one!"

"You like any woman!" Everyone in the group laughed. "Yes, Mike doesn't miss a beat, the Casanova."

"Yeah, just make fun of me, Mike will show you how it works. You'll all be amazed in the end. Watch out."

"What's he doing again?" Everyone in the group asked, and rightly so. He was always coming up with new ideas. He took a dog leash out of his navy overalls and played the desperate gentleman who had lost his dog. Mike made it so obvious that the two ladies at the bar noticed him. "What are you looking for?" asked the blonde woman. It seemed to work. "Well, I have a little poodle, he was my everything. He must have run away. I'm desperate. Would you like to be my noble lady?"

"That's outrageous. You don't know me at all, just smear your poodle somewhere else. Do you think this trick will work on me?"

"Well, maybe not with you, but possibly with your girlfriend? Who I think is prettier than you anyway." She gave him a slap, and his dog leash fell to the floor.

The two women left the bar because of Mike, the Casanova. Mike was devastated, and his cheek was red and throbbing. He held his hand to his cheek and picked up the dog leash.

"Who knows, perhaps next time it will work with the poodle attempt. Or he'll think of something new," I said loudly to the group. We doubled over with laughter.

We laughed so hard that a few glasses flew off the table.

Mike came to the table, and the barmaid had noticed that we had run out of drinks and wanted to provide us with new ones straight away. "A new round?"

"Of course, and this time it's all on our friend Mike, the one who lost his poodle."

"Would you like to be my noble lady?" Mike asked the barmaid. "Please what?" The barmaid gave Mike a slap and was visibly annoyed. "Please bring us another round, the same as before," I said and objected skillfully. "I'd love to!"

She smiled kindly at me. To my amazement, I was always the shy and reserved marine who was respected by the women. Maybe because I did less than Mike—much less, to be precise. Mike sat down next to me with a red cheek that was still throbbing a little.

I patted him on the shoulder. "Well, Casanova, you probably need to practice a bit more, I'll give you a tip, stick to the truth next time."

"Ha, ha, ha. Not everyone has as much supernatural charm as you and can just do nothing."

"Sometimes less is more."

"Mike, why don't you try a real dog or a baby carriage next time? Maybe that'll go down better."

"Right, guys, the next round is already here." The barmaid put our cocktails down… "Here's to good, successful times! Here's to every poodle finding its master."

Everyone laughed and drank their cocktails. When the fire show was over, a new singer was announced. We quietened down a little and turned our full attention to the stage.

The band was ready to start. But the singer was still missing. "Marlen, what's taking you so long? The audience is already waiting for you! It's your turn.

Please don't mess it up again like last time. I've already announced you."

"Yes, I only need another minute." Marlen took another deep breath and powdered her nose, but she just couldn't get her stage fright under control.

She touched up her red lipstick. Her chestnut-brown hair shimmered in the light. Her white sequin dress was perfect all around. She had no reason to be nervous. She was a wonderful singer.

Once again, she summoned up all her courage and put on her necklace. It always brought her luck. She went outside. The light was on her. The band had started to play. The audience was getting a little impatient.

"Tonight, I'd like to introduce you to Marlen, the wonderful singer who has already made her debut in New York on several big stages."

"Get on with it, great singer from New York!" A member of the audience shouted cheekily onto the stage. Everyone sitting at the table laughed with him. We continued to drink our cocktails and were curious to find out who Marlen was. And suddenly an apparition in white with many sequins on her dress came on stage.

She seemed a little nervous, shy, and beautiful at the same time. There was something graceful about her gait. I was impressed by her right from the start. Her chestnut brown hair shone in the spotlight.

The band did a second run-through when she started to sing. It was all over for me. I had fallen in love with Marlen right from the start. Head over heels, without saying a word to her beforehand.

I don't know what you call something like that—maybe that certain something or the chemistry between two people that crystallizes within seconds. That's how it was with me and Marlen. She gave me a look. The rest of the audience had also fallen silent.

Those who were still laughing before were quiet in the audience and blown away by Marlen, as I was. Her voice was as beautiful as she was. Her voice was as beautiful as she was. I whispered over to Mike. "That's my future wife." Mike looked at me irritated. "How do you know that? You haven't even said a word to her!"

"Call it intuition, I just know." When she had finished her performance, the audience applauded loudly. She thanked them, still looking a little shy and nervous. She walked off the stage, and I had lost sight of her. I had to act quickly before someone else could beat me to it. I kept an eye out for her, but she was nowhere to be seen.

Meanwhile, the band was playing another song, and people started dancing. There she was! She had changed into a light floral summer dress with a flower in her dark hair. She was talking to the barmaid who had brought the cocktails to our table earlier. I got up and wanted to go to the bar. Mike nudged me. "Here, the dog leash, you might need it if it doesn't work the normal way." Everyone laughed. "I think I'm more successful without you, but thank you, dear." I gave him his leash and walked to the bar where Marlen was sitting, drinking her cocktail.

I sat down inconspicuously next to her. And at least tried to keep up appearances. Then I ordered water to remain inconspicuous. A glance at her told me that she was lost in her thoughts. She was almost too perfect to be true. But she didn't even know how beautiful and perfect she was.

I wanted to speak to her and didn't dare. I looked back at our table. Everyone was watching me. Mike pointed to his dog leash again, and I just shook my head.

"Your friends seem to have been watching us for a while." I spilled my water. I hadn't expected her to speak to me. She took a towel from the bar and handed it to me. She smiled at me a little mischievously. I still couldn't get a word out. When Mike joined us. "My friend is the best soldier and comrade. That's the best match they could make of us weaklings. Another round of your best cocktails for us at the table!"

"I believe you, but how am I supposed to date someone who can't speak?" She laughed as she gave Mike an answer. "Yeah, our friend's a bit shy, just bear with him."

"Mike, enough already, didn't you want to go to the table? I have to apologize for my friend, he talks non-stop all day. Mostly nonsense, but he has a big heart and is one of my best friends. In case you haven't noticed, I'm the quieter one of the two of us. "I would never have noticed that!" She quipped. "You're not from here, are you?"

"No, we're here as soldiers on a mission, we were shipped here from the naval base and will be moving on tomorrow. We took a break to lift our spirits. We have our next deployment tomorrow."

"It sounds exciting and dangerous!"

"Well, of course we risk our lives every day, but for a good cause."

"Excuse me for saying that, I think risking your life is never good in that sense, whether for a good cause or a bad one. Excuse me, I have to get my things from the checkroom."

She left the bar and left me standing in the rain. I didn't dare look at my friends at the table, where everyone was already laughing with relish.

I didn't let it bother me and followed her into the cloakroom. "Miss Marlen, wait a minute, I haven't even properly introduced myself yet. My name is Richard. If I may say so, you are one of the most wonderful singers I have ever heard."

"Do you think so? Thank you very much. I'm always unhappy with my performance and always very nervous before every gig."

"If you'll allow me to meet you and invite you for a walk by the sea. There's another little bar right on the beach over there. We could walk there to stretch our legs a bit."

"I'm afraid they won't let up otherwise, will they?"

"I'm afraid not!"

"Then we should get going." I followed Marlen unobtrusively, and although she was so dismissive towards me, I knew for some inexplicable reason that she was the right woman for me. Her aura reminded me of the actresses in Hollywood films. She was beautiful and had something attractive about her that I couldn't put into words. It was a wonderful evening that I will never forget. I can still see it in my mind's eye as if it were yesterday. I quietly followed Marlen. The stars were shining in the sky, the bar wasn't that far away. I can still hear the sound of the sea in my ears. We walked along the beach. I wanted to break the icy silence. "Marlen, so you've already performed on New York stages?"

"Yes, actually, I've had a few gigs in New York. But unfortunately, I haven't made it to the big stage yet."

"I'm convinced that they will make it. I think they're great, if I may say so myself."

"Well, I do my best every day."

"So, you're booked to sing here?"

"Yes, for another six months, after that, I don't know where I'm going yet. Maybe I'll live with my relatives in New York for a while. We'll see."

"You can come and visit me!"

"Where exactly?"

"It's hard to say where this job will take me. I know it's a risky job, but I love it and pray every day that everything goes well on every mission. Of course, our fate is in God's hands, we can't control everything, even if we want to."

"I didn't mean to insult you like that earlier, sorry. I thought you were just trying to impress me and made up the story to appeal to me."

"Actually, I wanted to speak to you, but I didn't make anything up. Look, there's a shooting star, make a wish quickly! But please don't tell anyone. Otherwise, it won't come true." Marlen closed her eyes. She looked wonderful in the moonlight. She still had the flower in her dark hair. She opened her eyes. "I hope your wish comes true, all your wishes!"

She smiled at me for the first time. We decided not to go to the beach bar, and I walked her home instead. When will I see Marlen again? Maybe never again.

"Marlen, can I write to you?"

"Yes, I'll wait for it." She gave me a kiss on the cheek and closed the door. The flower she had in her hair was lying on the floor in front of the door. I picked it up and put it in my university jacket. I went to the beach bar to carefully put the flower away in a napkin.

The next few days were very eventful for us. We were shipped to Japan and had our mission there, where Mike, my best friend, died at the age of 23. We sat in our tents and drank tequila and said goodbye to Mike with this drinking ritual. It was raining outside, and I cried all night, as did my colleagues. We couldn't believe that life could slip out of our fingers so quickly.

He was a good man and an even better friend. I started writing letters to Marlen at night. I wrote to her every day and prayed that I would see her again soon. Furthermore, I realized that life is very short and that you shouldn't miss the opportunities you are given. You can't just let them pass you by. She replied to me promptly. I was the happiest man.

She told me how she had already announced that she was going to New York to live with her relatives. Likewise, she wanted to continue her career as a singer there. Unfortunately, as she sometimes wrote to me in her letters, things didn't turn out as she had initially hoped. Apart from a few gigs in small bars on the side street, no better offers had materialized for her as a singer.

I wanted to come and visit her in New York, and I did. I took a small bed and breakfast near her home. It was Christmastime in New York. Simply the most wonderful time of the year. It was like a fairy tale. Music was playing. The skating rink was open.

We also decided to go skating. Marlen wasn't good at it, so I held her by the hand. The ice rink was full of children and families. It was the best time of my life. When I held her hand, I never wanted to leave her again. We took a break and walked out of the rink. She began to tell me. "I have a job offer as a singer in Paris."

"Wow, Marlen, I'm happy for you!" "That's the job I've always wanted. I'm meeting an agent there who wants to help me with my career."

"You should go, but before you decide to go to Paris, please let me ask you one more question." I knelt down in front of Marlen, the people around us seemed to register it too.

"Wait, Richard, what are you doing?"

"Marlen, let me finish. Ever since I first saw you in that bar in Hawaii, I knew you were going to be my wife. My intuition didn't deceive me then. I want to spend my life with you, grow old with you, stick together in good times and bad, and love you until death do us part."

I took out the blue box containing the engagement ring I had bought it for Marlen.

"Marlen, will you be my wife?" Everyone looked over at Marlen with excitement. Marlen didn't know what to say.

I was either going to make a fool of myself or be the happiest man on earth.

"Since Mike, I've become even more aware that everything is so fleeting and that the perfect moment simply passes if you don't grab it. So, what's left to wait for? Become my wife!" Marlen hesitated briefly and then said out loud, YES! Everyone around us applauded loudly and congratulated us. It was an unforgettable moment. I put her engagement ring on Marlen, and we kissed.

The wedding was just a month later and we moved in together. I had a few more assignments, but then I changed jobs for Marlen's sake because the assignments were far too dangerous now that I was married to her.

I went into business for myself and became very successful. Marlen managed everything in the business. She never went to Paris … and gave up her career for my sake.

She turned down her agent in Paris. Inwardly I was relieved about it, of course, but sometimes I reproached myself for it, wondering what might have happened if she had gone to Paris as she had planned.

She had a few gigs, but she concentrated more on our business and family planning.

"Wow, I didn't know it was such a wonderful story with you and Grandma. Why didn't you ever tell me?"

"Well, I thought she'd bore you."

The fire was still flickering a little in the fireplace. Grandpa went to the drawer and took something out. He came back to the armchair and handed me a napkin. "Open it!" I slowly unfolded the napkin.

There was a dried flower. "This is the flower your grandma wore the night we first saw each other in Hawaii. I've kept it until today. Grandma doesn't know anything about it. But I was so convinced from the first moment that she was the right woman for me. I knew it from the very first moment."

I had tears in my eyes. "Grandpa, that's the best story I've ever heard, I didn't know Grandma could sing so beautifully."

"She hasn't sung for years. I sometimes regret that. But there's nothing I can do about that now. It's definitely too late for that."

"She had you for that, and that's the best thing that could have happened to her. Who knows if she had been successful in Paris? Nobody knows. Maybe you saved her from making a big mistake!"

"Possibly. Look, I still want to show you these pictures." Grandpa dug out a few pictures that were flying around in the photo album. "That was your grandma when she was young."

"Wow, she was beautiful, almost like an actress from Hollywood movies."

"That's Mike and me in Hawaii."

"You didn't do too bad yourself. Mike looks like he was a very cheerful person."

"He was one of my best friends, I'll never forget him. But now, enough of my boring old stories. Go to bed now, tomorrow is Christmas or today already. It's already 2 AM."

I was already tired. I gave my grandpa a kiss on the cheek and went to sleep. I dreamed of Hawaii, Rockefeller Center, Paris, and unfulfilled dreams.

The story made me a little sad. But I was already nervous because it was Christmas, and even though I wasn't 12 anymore, I was still hoping to get my PlayStation finally.

Christmas

The long wait was finally over. It was Christmas, and I could hardly wait to unwrap my presents. The sun was shining full force on my still somewhat sleepy face. Today was Christmas Eve, the best day of the year.
I opened the window to let in some fresh air. The snow was 30 cm high on the streets. A boy slipped in front of his house door. I had to smile a little. I quickly brushed my teeth, freshened up, and went to the dining area, but there was no one there.

Then I dashed into the kitchen, where I almost slipped. Sure enough, my grandma was standing in front of the stove, working on something for Christmas Eve. What would she make this time? As always, when my grandma was around, it smelled of Mandarins, Gingerbread, and oranges. That smell! It must have come from the cakes she made every hour.

"Are you ready? We have to go!"

"Where to?"

"To church, Melissa, darling, you overslept. It's already lunchtime, church starts soon."

"Yes, I was up very late last night. Grandpa told me a wonderful story."

"Yes, the storyteller, what has he come up with now?"
"Well, I'll just say Hawaii and the Rockefeller Center."

"He told you that? Oh, the nutcase." Grandma smiled to herself and grabbed her head. She had to sit down for a moment because she was feeling dizzy.

"Is everything okay? I'll give you a glass of water. You've just overdone it, the last few days. It was too much."

"Oh, I'm fine, I'm fine again." I quickly went to put on my best dress. My grandparents and I arrived at the church on time. Philipp was there with Grumpy, Marie-Therese with her parents, and the whole neighborhood, who were at my grandma's for pre-Christmas dinner. The choir sang, and everyone stood and clapped along. It was wonderful, it rounded off the day's before perfectly. Inside, I was still moved by my grandfather's story. I saw how they still loved each other after all the years they had been together. That was the meaning of Christmas for me! Not the presents, PlayStation, or cake. But the love for the people who are close to you. To reconcile and forget, and to love unconditionally. It started snowing again outside. When we got home, we kept to ourselves. My grandmother put the most beautiful cakes on the table, from chocolate cake to lemon meringue pie. There was no mention of the main course. I couldn't decide where to start. My grandfather was sipping his whiskey with relish, probably reminiscing about the old days. The fire in the fireplace flickered, a cozy feeling on my skin. The red boots were hanging by the stove, the Christmas tree was lit up brighter than ever before, and the bottom of the tree was full of presents. I hadn't even thought about the presents! Now I was a little nervous. It was getting on towards evening, and my grandparents and I were unwrapping the first packages. There was actually my PlayStation, 4 different games, and money. I was so happy. I gave my grandparents concert tickets, which they had always wanted. A successful Christmas Eve. I was slowly getting tired and wanted to go to bed. I gave my grandmother a kiss and hugged her. "Thank you for everything."

"Dear Melissa, I love you more than anything. Don't forget that!"

"I'll never forget that, Marlen, I love you too."

Christmas Day

*L*ast night I had a strange dream. I dreamt that I was standing outside in the snow, without socks, all alone and couldn't move as I wanted to. When I tried to run, I failed miserably. From a distance, I saw a small house with smoke coming out of the chimney. I was finally able to move my legs, I ran through the snow without socks, but I wasn't cold. It was a pleasant feeling all over my skin.

In the forest twilight, a deer jumped up, and I saw it running away. Slowly, I got closer to the house. I looked in the window and saw a slightly older woman who looked remarkably like my grandma. She was sitting in the armchair in front of the fireplace, crocheting socks for me.

The dream was so real that I could smell the scent of the forest. Then I woke up. A little startled, I looked at the blanket and then out of the window.

The snow seemed to be getting higher and higher so that the cars were completely snowed in. There were no people to be seen on the streets for miles around. Finally, I was able to collect myself to distinguish a dream from reality. The dream was so real.

What did it mean? I didn't think about it any further and went to the dining area. The tree had lost some of its luster today. I bent it down and poured some water so it wouldn't die of thirst. Funnily enough, there wasn't a soul around. Had my grandparents probably gone for a walk or to the neighbors?

Had I slept in all day again? Well, it is Christmas after all, so you deserve some time off. I put on my winter coat and went out to the garage to see if the car was there. Just as I thought, it was gone. It was freezing cold.

I was back in the house, munching on what was left of the lemon meringue pie. My grandma could really bake, but the fact that she could also sing was news to me.

The wonderful story was still in my subconscious. When suddenly the phone rang… I picked up the receiver. "Hello!" It was my grandpa on the phone. He was talking quickly and was very excited. I couldn't understand a single word. "Grandpa, please slow down, I can't understand what you're saying. Where are you?

I'm having a go at the lemon meringue pie." I continued to eat with relish and didn't let my grandfather spoil my great mood. Furthermore, I had been far too happy over the last few days and was still in my Christmas dream.

"Your grandma, your grandma."

"What about my grandma? Please tell her the cake is better than ever this time, she's outdone herself this time." My grandpa was silent at the end of the other line.

"What's wrong?"

"Your grandma, your grandma, passed away in the hospital this morning." I dropped my spoon and the cake on the floor. I couldn't believe what my grandpa had to say. The phone also flew to the floor.

I had tears in my eyes. The phone rang again. I picked up the phone.

"My darling, listen to me. There's a form in my drawer in the bedroom next to my bed that I really need. I'm going to stay in the hospital tonight, please bring me my things too."

I hung up the phone. In the bedroom, I looked in one drawer, then the next. Then I found what I was supposed to bring my grandpa. When I suddenly saw a postcard of Paris. The card was beautiful, I turned it over, and on it was a beautiful young woman in a white sequined dress.

I started to cry, there were tears on the card. I noticed the photos on the wall. In fact, my grandfather hadn't made up the story. Wonderful paintings from when my grandma was young. She was a beautiful woman. At that moment, I thought of the dream. I packed my things and called a cab to take me to the hospital. Tears were streaming down my face. I had the Paris postcard in my jacket pocket.

Boxing Day

When my grandfather and I arrived home from the hospital, the house seemed very deserted and empty. We put our things down and were both disoriented at first.

My grandfather went to the fireplace and lit it to warm up the house a little. He switched on the Christmas tree lights and sat down in the armchair. We didn't say a word. I went into the kitchen to make us breakfast, the kitchen was so empty and loveless without my grandma cooking for us.

I imagined her at the stove saying: "Melissa, my darling, you've slept through most of the day again. Come on, get ready. The guests are about to arrive."

Tears were streaming down my face, but I had to be strong for my grandpa. He was now alone in this big, beautiful house. But my grandma was missing. Back at my grandpa's, I saw him sitting still by the fireplace.

I had never seen him so thoughtful. I sat down next to him and held his hand. He was crying. It broke my heart. We looked at the fireplace in silence and watched the soft flickering of the stove. It was so calming.

Tears were running down my cheeks too. I remembered that I had wrapped the Paris Post card in my winter coat.

I picked it up and placed it on the back of the chair. My grandpa took it in his hand and smiled. "Where did you find this?"

"In the cupboard when I was looking for the form. I hope you're not angry with me for taking it with me."

"But no, I'd already forgotten them. My darling, Grandma, had been ill for a while. We didn't tell you because we would rather not burden you."

"You wouldn't have burdened me. It was the most wonderful Christmas I have ever had, and I will be forever grateful for that. I will never forget it!" I held his hand, and we didn't say another word. The house was incredibly quiet.

I had never experienced it like this before. You could even hear the snow falling from the roof.

The front doorbell rang. I only responded after the second ring. I grabbed Grandpa by the shoulder and said: "I'll get it!" He nodded silently. I opened the door.

All the neighbors, including Marie-Therese, her parents, Philipp, and Grumpy, were standing in front of the door. There were about 20–30 people. The whole neighborhood.

I wiped the tears from my face and had a little smile. Grandpa didn't move from his chair.

"We've all brought something. We heard about your grandma. She was the most incredible woman we ever knew. We wanted to remember her like this on Boxing Day. We thought you could use some company." Grumpy wriggled around my feet and ran into the house. He stopped at Grandpa's. Grandpa stroked him on the head. "Thank you, Marie-Therese, of course you are all very welcome. Please come in." Everyone went into the house. They took off their winter coats and, in a subdued mood, brought some life back into the house.

Everyone brought cake and food. Grandpa still didn't move. He continued to stare at the fireplace. The people helped a little to cope with the situation. Everyone ate, including Grandpa and me. But nobody said a word.

Grandpa broke the silence when he played an old record. It was music from the 1950s.

The record that my grandma had recorded in New York. My grandpa had tears in his eyes, the Paris postcard was on the table. It was a good mood. Melancholy and cheerful at the same time.

This was how they wanted to remember the days they had spent with my grandma. My gaze went to the Christmas tree.

My grandma was pictured before my eyes again, running back and forth from the kitchen to the dining area to make everything perfect.

Sitting at the table, I rarely saw her. Grumpy came sidling around my legs again, growling something. I didn't know what was wrong, maybe he needed to go out.

Philip spoke to me, "Melissa, I think he's thirsty, would you give him a drink, or should I go?"

"No, it's okay, I'm going." I walked slowly into the kitchen to get the water for Grumpy. After all, I didn't want the poor guy to die of thirst. As I felt some water in the bowl, a scent seemed very familiar. It smelled of mandarins, gingerbread, and oranges. How I loved that scent.

Every year, the whole house smelled of it when I visited my grandparents. I had understood the meaning of Christmas. It's not the presents, the tree, or the Christmas decorations that make the holiday so special. It's the people who make it special. The whole year should be Christmas…

And I could still see my grandmother standing at the stove,
making the icing for the lemon meringue…